Dewdrop Fairies

Up, Up and Away

Patricia MacCarthy

PICTURE CORGI

It's just the right sort of warm windy
day for kite-flying.

It's just the right sort of warm
day for kite-flying.

JP

Buttercup and Poppy have made a beautiful petal kite, with a long flowing tail.

"It's like a brightly coloured dragon!" smiles Poppy.

"Let's go and fly it right now," says Buttercup.

The two Dewdrop Fairies race up the hill, trailing the dragon's tail behind them.

Holding the kite up high above her head,
Buttercup runs down the hill.

But when she lets go, the kite flops onto the grass.

It's Poppy's turn now – she is sure
she will do better than Buttercup.

But before she gets a chance to
have her go, Buttercup picks
up the kite and tries again . . .

and again . . .

and again.

"This silly kite won't fly!" Buttercup shouts crossly, flinging it to the ground.

Just then, a sudden gust of wind lifts it up
and off goes the kite, twirling into the sky.

Buttercup and Poppy watch in horror as the kite swoops and swerves . . .

and lands in a tall prickly bush.
Now Poppy is cross too.

"It's all your fault, Buttercup. You've ruined our kite.
This wouldn't have happened if you'd let me have a go."

"I'm sorry, Poppy," says Buttercup glumly.
"What are we going to do?"

Bluebell and Violet hear the commotion and come running.
"Whatever's the matter?" they ask.

Buttercup points to the kite.

"Our kite has got stuck and we can't reach it," she wails.

"And it's all prickly up there," adds Poppy.

"I've got an idea," says Violet. "Fetch the others!"

The Dewdrop Fairies gather together
and Violet explains her plan.

They form a pyramid with Rose at the top.
She's very good with thorns!

"Don't wobble!" she calls.

Rose manages to
untangle the kite
without pricking
herself.

"Thank you, Rose, thank you, everyone," says Buttercup.
"Now Poppy can fly the kite – it IS her turn, after all."
"Thank you, Buttercup," smiles Poppy.

Poppy runs with the kite. The others follow, willing
the kite to fly.

They run and run and run, until . . .

. . . up, up and away goes the twisting, twirling kite, carried by the wind.

"Wow! Our dragon really is flying!" laughs Buttercup,
as Poppy holds on tight to the kite string.
"Who wants a go next?"

"Me, please," calls Violet.

"Then me," says Waterlily.

"I want to go next!" replies Rose.

For Jean and Jim,
my mother and father

UP, UP AND AWAY
A PICTURE CORGI BOOK 978 0 552 55754 2

First published in Great Britain by Picture Corgi,
an imprint of Random House Children's Books
A Random House Group Company

This edition published 2009

1 3 5 7 9 10 8 6 4 2

Text copyright © Random House Children's Books, 2009
Illustrations copyright © Patricia MacCarthy, 2009
Concept © Random House Children's Books and Patricia MacCarthy, 2009
Text by Alison Ritchie
Design by Tracey Cunnell

The right of Patricia MacCarthy to be identified as the illustrator of this work
has been asserted in accordance with the Copyright, Designs and Patents Act 1988.

Picture Corgi Books are published by Random House Children's Books,
61-63 Uxbridge Road, London W5 5SA

www.dewdropfairies.com
www.rbooks.co.uk

Addresses for companies within The Random House Group Limited
can be found at: www.randomhouse.co.uk/offices.htm

THE RANDOM HOUSE GROUP Limited Reg. No. 954009

A CIP catalogue record for this book is available from the British Library.

Printed in China